Ladybug Garden

Fitzhenry & Whiteside
195 Allstate Parkway
Markham, Ontario   L3R 4T8

Acknowledgments
The Author wishes to thank Pat MacCulloch, Entomologist with the Royal Ontario Museum, and Gord Grant, Apiary Specialist with the Ministry of Agriculture and Food, for graciously giving of their time and counsel.

Canadian Cataloguing in Publication Data

Godkin, Celia.
    Ladybug garden

ISBN 1–55041–083–0

1. Garden ecology – Juvenile literature. 2. Garden pests – Biological control – Juvenile literature.
I. Title.

QH541.5.G37G6 1994   j574.5'264   C94–932198–2

Printed in Canada

95 96 97 98 99 FP 6 5 4 3 2 1

For my family

The gardener looked all around his garden,
and he liked what he saw.
There were hardy vegetables, brightly colored flowers,
and fruit trees that made the air smell sweet.
There were many kinds of insects in the garden, too:
ladybugs and wasps, bees and butterflies, aphids and ants.

The gardener thought about all those insects.
He knew that bees and butterflies helped the garden grow.
As they flew from flower to flower, drinking nectar,
they picked up a fine yellow dust called pollen,
which the flowers produced.
By carrying pollen from one flower to another,
the bees and butterflies helped the flowers
produce seeds for new plants.

Though the butterflies were helpful, the gardener knew
that their young — the caterpillars — were not.
They often damaged plants by eating the leaves.

The ants and wasps in the garden
were harmful in one way but helpful in another.
They sometimes nibbled on ripe fruit
before the gardener got around to picking it.
But they also helped the garden by eating harmful insects.

There was no question about the aphids, though.
The gardener knew they were bad for the garden,
because they sucked plant juices and spread diseases.

He didn't know much about the bright red ladybugs,
but he thought they were special and was very fond of them.

One day the gardener had an idea.
If I get rid of the bad insects, he thought,
my garden will be perfect.
So the next day, the gardener sprayed the fruit trees,
the vegetables, and the flowers.
He used a spray gun filled with bug killer.

As the gardener sprayed the poison,
the bees, ants, and wasps
hid in their nests to protect themselves.
But the ladybugs didn't have any nests,
so they flew away in a great red cloud.

The aphids didn't have nests either,
but, without wings, they couldn't fly away.
They hid under the leaves in the garden.

When the gardener finished spraying,
the aphids crept out of their hiding places
and went back to work.
Many of them died from the poison,
but others survived.

The aphids sucked the juice
out of leaves and tender plant stems.
Some of the juice passed through their bodies
and turned into a sweet, sticky liquid called honeydew.

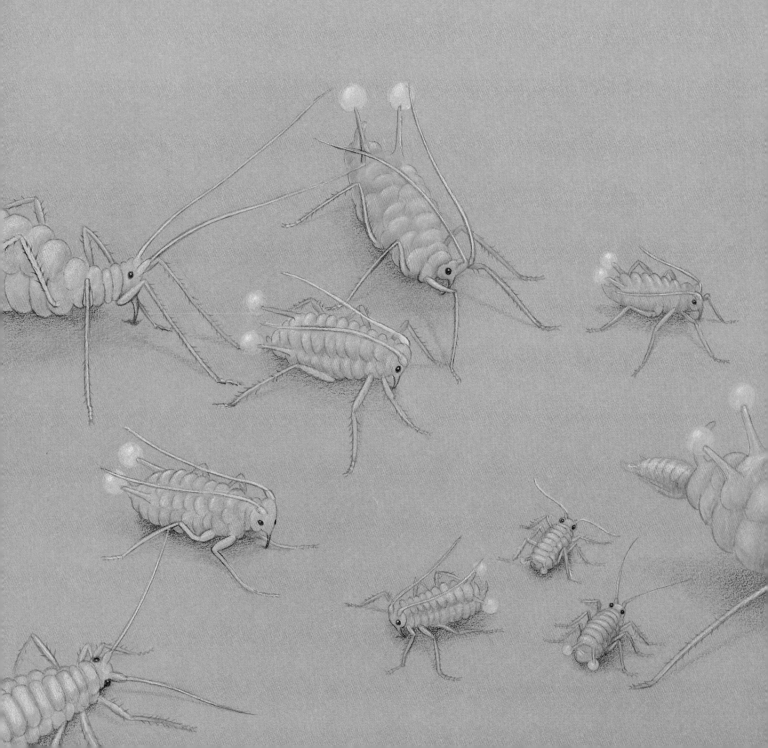

Soon it seemed there were more aphids than ever before.
As they multiplied, they sucked more and more plant juice.
It wasn't long before the plants in the garden
were coated with sticky honeydew, which ants love.

The ants "milked" the aphids
by stroking them with their feelers.
This made the aphids
squeeze out honeydew,
which the ants then licked up.

There were so many ants
going to get honeydew from the aphids
that the gardener began to see ant trails
all over the garden.

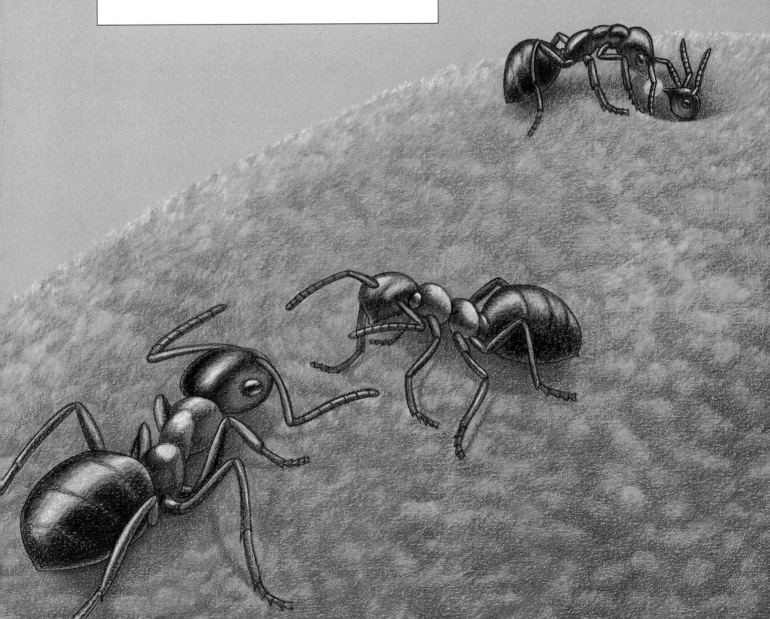

The bees in the garden liked honeydew, too.
It was easier for the bees to lick honeydew
from the plants to make their honey
than it was for them to go
from flower to flower collecting nectar.
Besides, there were fewer flowers now.
The plants had become too sick to make many flowers,
because of the damage the aphids had done.

With fewer flowers, there were
fewer butterflies visiting the garden.
But there were still many caterpillars.
They stayed in the garden, eating leaves,
until they grew big enough
to turn into butterflies and fly away.

Not only were the plants too sick to make many flowers,
the fruit trees were too sick to produce much fruit.
Wasps buzzed angrily about,
fighting over what little fruit there was.

And all the while,
the aphids continued to multiply.
There were so many, in fact,
that they were crowded together on the plants,
fighting one another for food and space.
Many plants were so covered with honeydew
that they grew moldy.

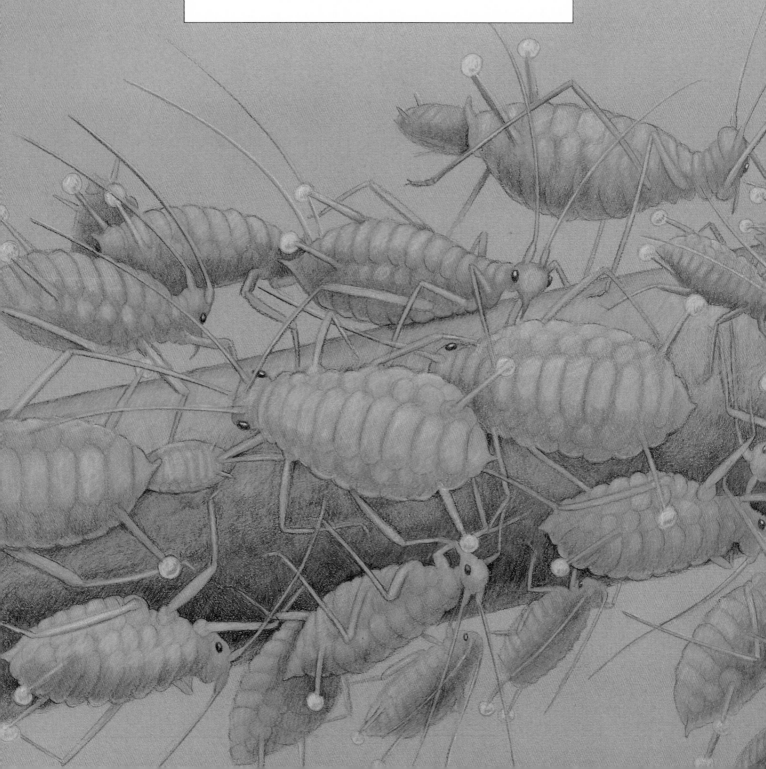

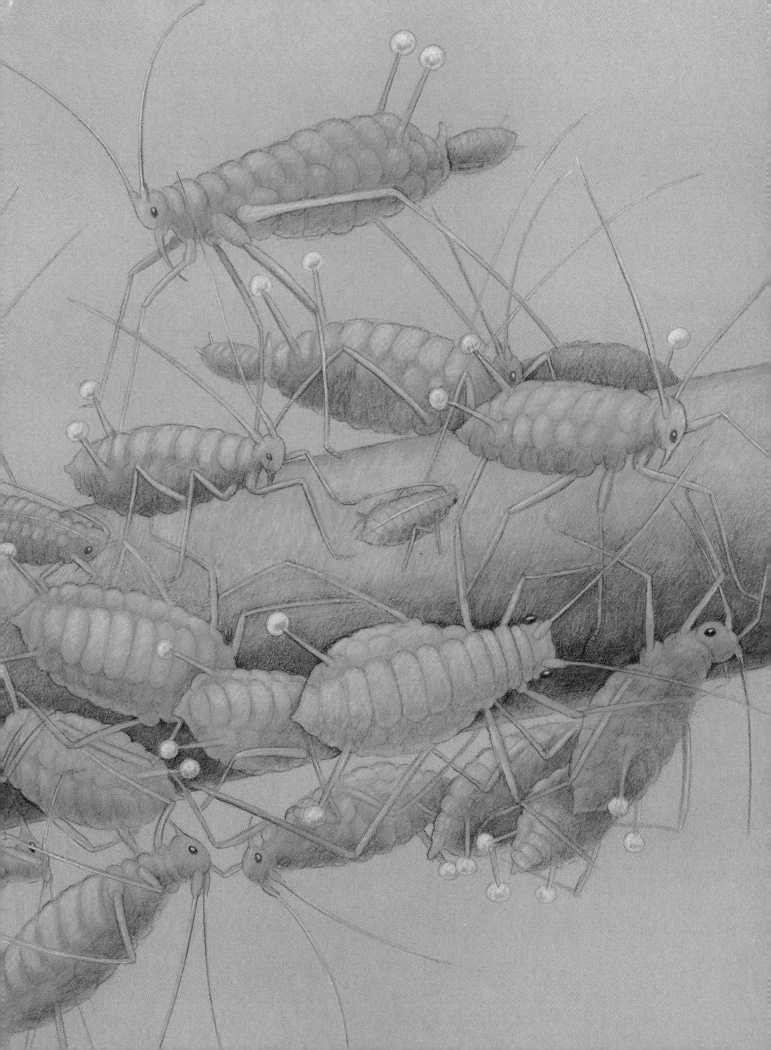

The gardener knew that something was terribly wrong.
The garden had few flowers, the fruit trees had little fruit,
and the vegetables were shriveled up and wilted.
The plants were covered with aphids.
There were ant hills and ant trails everywhere.
The wasps were becoming a nuisance,
and the butterflies had all but disappeared.
Even the bees' honey tasted strange, because they
had made it from honeydew instead of nectar.

The gardener didn't know what to do.
He could see that spraying
with poison had been a mistake.
He understood now
that all the life in his garden
was linked somehow,
that the plants and insects
depended on one another to survive.

"What about ladybugs?" a friend suggested.
"What about them?" the gardener asked.
"Ladybugs are nature's way
of controlling aphids," the friend replied.
And she gave him an address
from which to order a supply.

When the box of ladybugs arrived,
the gardener took it out to the garden,
opened it, and left it in a shady spot under a tree.
One by one, the ladybugs flew or crawled out of the box.
Soon they were all over the garden.

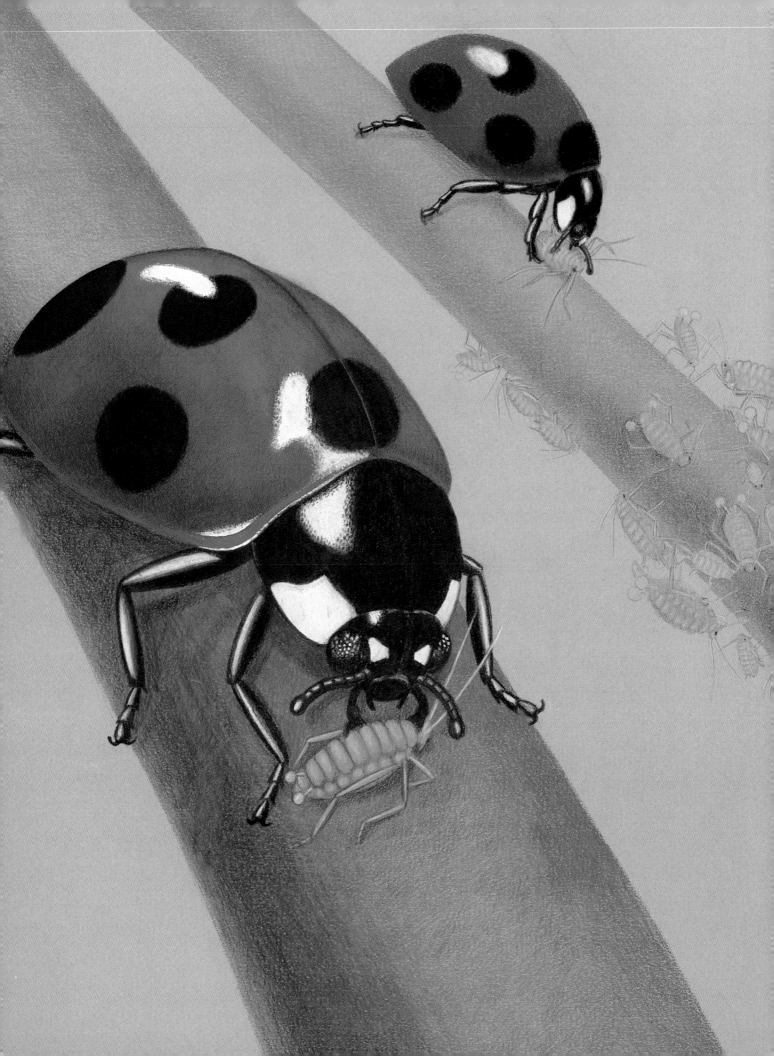

The ladybugs ate all the aphids they could find.
They ate and ate and ate and ate.
And after a while, the garden began to recover.
The plants grew stronger and healthier.